YASMIN

The Singer

written by
SAADIA FARUQI

illustrated by
HATEM ALY

PICTURE WINDOW BOOKS
a capstone imprint

To Mariam for inspiring me, and Mubashir
for helping me find the right words—S.F.

To my sister, Eman, and her amazing girls,
Jana and Kenzi—H.A.

Yasmin is published by Picture Window Books, an imprint of Capstone.
1710 Roe Crest Drive
North Mankato, Minnesota 56003
www.capstonepub.com

Text copyright © 2021 by Saadia Faruqi.
Illustrations copyright © 2021 by Capstone.

Library of Congress Cataloging-in-Publication Data is available on the
Library of Congress website.
Names: Faruqi, Saadia, author. | Aly, Hatem, illustrator. Title: Yasmin
the singer / written by Saadia Faruqi ; illustrated by Hatem Aly.
Description: North Mankato, Minnesota : Picture Window Books,
[2021] | Series: Yasmin | Audience: Ages 5-7. | Audience: Grades K-1.
| Summary: Yasmin is excited to attend a wedding party, but when
the singing starts Yasmin is too shy to join in. Identifiers: LCCN
2020039023 (print) | LCCN 2020039024 (ebook) | ISBN 9781515882626
(hardcover) | ISBN 9781515883753 (paperback) | ISBN 9781515892526
(pdf) | ISBN 9781515893288 (kindle edition) Subjects: CYAC:
Bashfulness—Fiction. | Pakistani Americans—Fiction. | Muslims—United
States—Fiction. Classification: LCC PZ7.1.F373 Yiw 2021 (print) | LCC
PZ7.1.F373 (ebook) | DDC [E]—dc23 LC record available at https://
lccn.loc.gov/2020039023 LC ebook record available at https://lccn.loc.
gov/2020039024

Editorial Credits:
Editor: Kristen Mohn; Designer: Kay Fraser; Production Specialist: Tori
Abraham

Design Elements:
Shutterstock: LiukasArt

TABLE OF CONTENTS

CHAPTER 1

A Party

It was a very special evening. Yasmin, Mama, and Nani were going to a party.

Yasmin loved wearing her Pakistani shalwar kameez.

"You look wonderful!" Baba exclaimed.

"Thank you," Yasmin replied.

"I think he's talking to me, jaan!" Nani teased.

The party was at Aunt Zara's house. Her friend was getting married.

"Salaam!" Aunt Zara said. "You're going to have so much fun, Yasmin!"

Yasmin felt shy as they entered the house.

There were so many people in the room. Their clothes were colorful. Their jewelry sparkled.

The bride was dressed in the most beautiful clothes. Yasmin couldn't stop staring at her.

Mama pointed to a woman sitting across the room.

"Want to put on some henna, Yasmin?" Mama asked.

"Will you come with me?" Yasmin asked.

Mama nodded.

The woman painted a pretty
design on Yasmin's hand.

"It matches my dress,
Mama," Yasmin whispered.

Mama smiled. "It certainly
does!"

They ate delicious food and
walked around the room.

"Why don't you go play with
the kids?" Mama suggested.

Yasmin shook her head. She
wanted to stay close to Mama.

CHAPTER 2

Sing a Song with Me

After dinner, a group of girls sat on the floor. They played a dholki and clapped their hands. They laughed and sang songs in Urdu with happy voices.

The other guests sat around them, listening. Smiling.

Mama knew the words to the song. "You know this one too, Yasmin. Sing with us!"

"No, thanks," Yasmin mumbled.

She felt like everyone was looking at her.

Yasmin got up and walked

quietly to the side of the room.

She just wanted to be alone.

Nani waved to her. "Come here, jaan," she called. But Yasmin shook her head. She was just fine in the corner.

Next to her was a pretty silk curtain. Yasmin slid behind it and sat down.

That was better! Now nobody could see her. Yasmin listened to the song and felt her heart jump. Mama was right. She did know this one!

Soon, Yasmin was singing too. It was just a whisper, but that was okay. She sang softly, just to herself. It made her happy. It was a song about a bride, about beautiful clothes, and about henna.

Yasmin sang and sang.

CHAPTER 3

An Audience

Yasmin's voice got louder. She stood up. She imagined she was on a stage. The music was all around her, happy and loud.

She struck a pose. She flipped her head. She held up a pretend microphone.

Yasmin was so busy singing,
she didn't see what she was
doing. Her arm caught in the
curtain. Before she could catch it,
the curtain dropped to the floor.

Yasmin turned around. She stopped singing. Everyone in the room was looking at her.

"Oops," she whispered.

The girls on the floor were still drumming on the dholki, but they weren't singing.

They were all watching Yasmin. And they were all smiling. Then they started to clap!

Mama and Nani were smiling too.

Mama walked up and held
out her hand.

"Your voice is lovely,
jaan. Come join us. Let's sing
together!"

Yasmin took Mama's hand. It was okay. She was ready to sing with the others.

Think About It, Talk About It

✽ Have you ever been shy around other people? Did it keep you from doing something you wanted to do?

✽ Imagine you are Yasmin's friend. How you would give her courage if she was feeling nervous about something?

✽ Have you been to a special party or event where you got to dress up? If you could wear whatever you wanted, what would it be? Draw a picture.

✽ Is there a special type of music or song that makes you happy? What is it?

Learn Urdu with Yasmin!

Yasmin's family speaks both English and Urdu. Urdu is a language from Pakistan. Maybe you already know some Urdu words!

baba (BAH-bah)—father

dholki (DOL-kee)—a two-headed drum used with traditional Pakistani songs

henna (HEN-ah)—red or brown dye used to draw designs on the skin that will fade away

jaan (jahn)—life; a sweet nickname for a loved one

kameez (kuh-MEEZ)—long tunic or shirt

kitaab (kee-TAHB)—book

nani (NAH-nee)—grandmother on mother's side

salaam (sah-LAHM)—hello

shalwar (shahl-WAHR)—loose trousers worn under a kameez

Pakistan Fun Facts

Yasmin and her family are proud of their Pakistani culture. Yasmin loves to share facts about Pakistan!

Islamabad

PAKISTAN

Pakistan is on the continent of Asia, with India on one side and Afghanistan on the other.

Many languages are spoken in Pakistan, including Urdu, English, Saraiki, Punjabi, Pashto, Sindhi, and Balochi.

A famous, award-winning singer in Pakistan is Abida Parveen.

Each region of Pakistan has its own traditional music and instruments.

Pakistan adopted its national anthem in 1954 after a nationwide competition.

Make a Microphone

SUPPLIES:
- toilet paper roll
- foam paintbrush
- assorted paint colors
- large sheet of aluminum foil
- stickers or gemstones
- craft glue

STEPS:

1. Paint the toilet paper roll in your choice of color. After it's dry, paint on a second coat of the same color. Allow to dry completely.

2. Crumple up the aluminum foil into a ball shape.

3. Decorate the toilet roll with stickers or gemstones. Make sure to leave plenty of space for your hand to hold the microphone.

4. Carefully place craft glue around the top inside edge of the toilet paper roll.

5. Place the foil ball on top of the glue and allow it to set.

Saadia Faruqi is a Pakistani American writer, interfaith activist, and cultural sensitivity trainer featured in *O Magazine*. She is author of two middle grade novels, *A Place at the Table* and *A Thousand Questions*. She is also editor-in-chief of *Blue Minaret*, an online magazine of poetry, short stories, and art. Besides writing books, she also loves reading, binge-watching her favorite shows, and taking naps. She lives in Houston, Texas, with her husband and children.

Hatem Aly is an Egyptian-born illustrator whose work has been published all over the world. He currently lives in beautiful New Brunswick, Canada, with his wife, son, and more pets than people. When he is not dipping cookies in a cup of tea or staring at blank pieces of paper, he is usually drawing, reading, or daydreaming. You can see his art in books that earned multiple starred reviews and positions on the *NYT* Best-Sellers list, such as *The Proudest Blue* (with Ibtihaj Muhammad & S.K. Ali) and *The Inquisitor's Tale* (with Adam Gidwitz), a Newbery Honor winner.

Join Yasmin
on all her adventures!

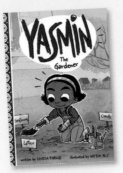
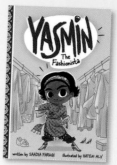

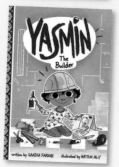